A SIERRA THE SEARCH DOG NOVEL

BRYCE BUMPS HIS HEAD

Josue —
Stay found!!

ROBERT D. CALKINS

Illustrated by Taillefer Long

Sierra the Search Dog Series

A SIERRA THE SEARCH DOG NOVEL

BRYCE BUMPS HIS HEAD

Bryce Bumps His Head
A Sierra the Search Dog Novel

By Robert D. Calkins

Callout Press

Published by Callout Press, Olalla, Washington, U.S.A.
Copyright © 2017 Robert Calkins
All rights reserved.

Developmental and Copy Editor: Lisa Canfield,
www.copycoachlisa.com

Illustration and Design: Taillefer Long, Illuminated Stories,
www.illuminatedstories.com

ISBN: 978-0-9971911-1-0
Library of Congress Control Number: 2016919699

DEDICATION

This book is dedicated to all of the Search and Rescue volunteers, dog handlers and dogs who respond in all weather and any terrain, at any time, so that others might live.

Contents

THE TEN ESSENTIALS

1. Navigation (map & compass)
2. Hydration (water & filter/purifier)
3. Nutrition (extra food)
4. Raingear and insulation
5. Firestarter
6. First Aid kit
7. Tools (knife or multi-tool)
8. Illumination (light, with extra batteries)
9. Sun Protection (sunscreen, sunglasses)
10. Shelter (tarp, rope and stakes)

CHAPTER 1
PLAY BOW

Little Nancy had gone missing–sort of. She was hiding in the bushes outside her house, waiting for Sierra and Bryce to find her. Sierra, a beautiful golden retriever, was also a search and rescue dog.

Nancy was hiding because Sierra needed to practice finding people.

Search and rescue is important work. At just 15, Bryce was the youngest SAR (short for search and rescue) dog handler in Washington state. He practiced with Sierra a lot. Bryce's father had told him, "Someone's life might depend on you someday. If you and Sierra are going to call yourselves a search and rescue team, then you need to put in the effort." He wanted to inspire Bryce and his dog to do their best.

Nancy had hidden between two big bushes where nobody could see her. But Bryce knew where she was. That wasn't cheating. Because this was practice, it was important for Bryce to know where Nancy was hiding, so he could learn how Sierra behaved when she picked up Nancy's scent.

Dogs and people are very different, especially when they're trying to find something, or someone. People use their eyes to look for what they want. When dogs want to find something, they mostly use their noses. Dogs can easily smell things that people can't. When they find what they're looking for, they say so through body language.

Sierra walked through the neighborhood sniffing the grass and the flowers and the bushes. The neighbors looked from their windows and saw that Bryce and Sierra were practicing. Sierra wore the spiffy "Search" vest she'd earned after the first time she found a missing little girl.

Bryce paid attention to which way the wind was blowing. After a few minutes of searching, he walked to a place downwind from Nancy's hiding spot. He needed to get Sierra's nose to a spot where the wind would carry Nancy's scent.

They were three houses away from Nancy when suddenly, Sierra's head snapped in just the right direction. That was Sierra's body language. It meant she smelled…something.

"Good girl. Let's find Nancy." Bryce said gently. Sierra hadn't found Nancy yet, but was starting to get a few whiffs of her. The dog turned and trotted in the direction of Nancy's house, moving back and forth as she went.

Bryce could see that Sierra was making her way right toward Nancy. This was shaping up to be another great practice session.

Suddenly, Bryce heard what sounded like a horse running up behind them. He looked, and saw that Rusty the Great Dane had gotten loose from the neighbor's house. Great Danes are one of the biggest dog breeds, and when they run it really does sound like a horse.

Rusty had seen Sierra from the window and pushed his way out the back door to join her. He was twice Sierra's size, but the two were best buddies. Bryce would frequently take Sierra over to Rusty's house so the two could romp in the family's fenced back yard.

Rusty bumped Bryce as he ran toward Sierra, knocking Bryce flat! Rusty wasn't being bad, he just really, really, wanted to play with his girlfriend Sierra.

Sierra was having none of it. She was working, and stayed focused on finding Nancy. It was like she didn't even know Rusty, who on any other day was her best doggie friend.

Rusty started whining. He really wanted to play! But Sierra kept walking toward Nancy. Bryce got back up to follow.

Rusty did not give up. He got down in front of Sierra and gave her what's called a "play bow." This is another way dogs use body language. When a dog wants to play with another dog, they can't just say "Want to play?" Rusty stretched out his front legs, lowered his shoulders until his chin was almost on the ground, and looked directly at Sierra. His mouth was open and his tongue was out, almost as if he was smiling. His rear end was way up in the air with his tail wagging.

It's the universal doggie body language for "Want to play?"

Sierra continued to ignore her best friend. She was doing important work, finding a missing person. This was not the time to play around.

Rusty rolled over. He raised both feet in the air and scratched his back on the grass. This was how he and Sierra would play together when they romped in his back yard.

But Sierra just kept following her nose toward Nancy.

Bryce decided not to interfere or try to stop the big Great Dane. A strange dog might come up to Sierra during a real search, and Bryce wanted to see how she'd handle it.

Now Rusty was running in circles and occasionally jumping up in the air, the same way he did when he and Sierra romped around Rusty's back yard. Except Rusty was the only one romping. Sierra was working.

The scene continued all the way to the bushes where Nancy was hiding. She heard the noise, and peeked out to see what was going on. She wasn't sure what would happen when Bryce and the two dogs got to her, but she ducked back down and waited to find out.

Finally, Sierra got to the bushes where Nancy was hiding. She looked in and saw Nancy, tagged her gently with one paw, and turned around. Then she ran as fast as she could towards Bryce and skidded to a halt right in front of him. She went into a perfect "sit" position, which was Sierra's body language for "Found her!"

Bryce replied by saying, "Show me!" and Sierra led him all the way back to Nancy.

Rusty stood to the side, watching the action, not understanding what just happened. His best friend completely ignored him, stuck her head in the bushes, ran back to the two-legged guy and sat down. Now Sierra was getting something he'd never seen her play with before–a bright orange ball.

Rusty didn't know that the ball was Sierra's favorite toy, and she only got it when she found a missing person. It was her "paycheck" for doing a good job on her search. Bryce and Nancy also scratched Sierra's back and rubbed her belly. The rubber ball made a squeaky sound while Sierra chewed on it.

Poor Rusty felt completely left out of the action. He laid down and wondered what was going on.

Finally, after Sierra played with her ball for a bit, Bryce knelt down next to her and took it from her. He also removed her vest. This is how Bryce told her that they were done searching.

Removing the vest was like flipping a switch. Sierra was no longer a search dog, she was just a dog. She was a dog whose best doggie friend was a few feet away and ready to play.

Once again Bryce ended up flat on the ground—this time because Sierra tried to jump over him to get to her friend Rusty. She ran up to the big dog, gave him a play bow, and off they went. First Sierra chased Rusty, then Rusty spun around and chased Sierra. They laid down next to each other and scratched their backs on the tall grass. There were eight doggie legs straight up in the air while they wriggled around!

"I watched Sierra ignore Rusty while she was trying to find me," Nancy said to Bryce. "That must have been hard."

"When Sierra is trying to find someone, not much gets in her way," Bryce replied. "Now it's time for her to let Rusty know they're still friends. We'll let them play for a while, and then......Sierrrrra......noooo!"

Sierra and Rusty had found the best thing ever. The two were splashing around in a gigantic mud puddle, and getting filthy. Sierra came out of the puddle covered in so much mud she looked like a completely different breed of dog.

"When we left the house an hour ago she was a golden retriever," Bryce said to Nancy. "I guess she'll be going home as a chocolate lab."

CHAPTER 2
COUNT OFF!

Heather James, leader of Girl Scout Troop 36, had almost decided to cancel the hike. The weather forecast was bad and a number of girls had already dropped out. Mrs. James made a list of those who were still coming, and realized they were the most active girls in the troop. These were exactly the people she wanted to take on the hike. She knew they'd learn the most from being in the woods in bad weather.

Mrs. James had been a Girl Scout leader for as long as she could remember. Some of the girls she'd helped had grown up, and now they were leading scout troops of their own.

"Anybody can hike in good weather," Mrs. James thought. "We'll make this an adventure in staying warm and dry."

She called every parent whose daughter was still coming.

"It'll be wet and cold," she told each one. "I can teach the girls how to be safe and have fun in the rain, but they do need to dress properly. No cotton, and especially not jeans. Once cotton gets wet it stays wet, and sucks the heat right out of you!"

The girls who were coming were the most prepared in the troop. As Girl Scouts, they'd "scouted" Goodwill, St. Vincent dePaul, and every other second-hand store in the city. They'd found some very nice used hiking gear without paying too much. Part of being a Girl Scout was learning to be careful with money, and shopping for deals was fun.

They met at the trail head, and before their parents drove off, Mrs. James checked to make sure each girl was properly equipped. They were all wearing real hiking clothing, and they each had a small backpack with nine of the Ten Essentials.

"I'm so impressed!" Mrs. James told the group. "My job is to help you be safe, but every one of you came prepared today. It's going to be wet and cold out there, but we're going to have a great time."

The girls paired up with hiking partners, so that even if they hiked at different speeds, nobody would be alone. The troop might spread out along the trail, but everyone would have a buddy with them in case something happened.

Before leaving the trail head, Mrs. James also taught them something called "counting off." If the team leader can't see everybody, they holler "Count off!!" and everyone yells their number in order. If somebody doesn't holler back, the rest of the team goes to look for them.

"Okay girls, line up," she said. "Betsy, I want you to start off as number one. Then Rochelle is number two, Diane is number three and right on down the line. Ready? Let's give it a try."

Mrs. James didn't know the girls had already learned to count off in gym class at school.

"ONE!!" yelled Betsy.

"TWOOOO!" Rochelle cried, even louder.

"Three." Diane said. Diane was the quietest girl in school, and she just wasn't used to yelling about anything.

"You're going to have to be much louder than that," Mrs. James explained gently. "It's not rude to yell when you're calling out your number. It's about your safety, so we need to hear you."

"THREEEEEE!!" Diane yelled, scaring everybody. No one had ever heard her be that loud before.

Betsy was the first to recover from the shock. "Wow, Diane, remind me never to make you mad," she said. "I didn't know you had that in you."

"Yes, that was nice!" Mrs. James coached. "Remember to be that loud when we count off for real."

As a final step before starting the hike, Mrs. James gave each team member a map of the area in a clear plastic bag. That completed their list of the Ten Essentials. Then everyone went over the map to make sure they all knew their starting point and where they were going.

"Okay, girls, we're off," Mrs. James said. "Remember what I told you at our last meeting. Don't worry about keeping up with the people ahead of you. The trick is to not lose the people behind you. If you start losing sight of the girls behind you, just slow down. The team ahead of you will see that you've slowed down, and that way we'll all stay in sight of each other."

The rain was coming harder now. It was so loud hitting the trees Mrs. James knew it would be difficult to hear each other when they counted off. She wanted to make sure they practiced, so after only about five minutes of hiking, she hollered "Count off!!"

"ONE!" yelled Betsy.

"TWO!" cried Rochelle.

"THREEEEEE!!!" screamed Diane, remembering to give it her best shot.

And so it went, on down to Dana, who was number 14. She yelled loud enough that Mrs. James could hear her up at the front of the line, and then everyone resumed hiking.

Dana was the explorer of the group. She wasn't the slowest hiker, but she was the person who wanted to check out all the side trails. Some were on the map, but some weren't. Those were the ones she most wanted to visit. Her hiking partner Jan hissed at her.

"You're going to slow everybody down. We can ask Mrs. James if we can check out those trails on the way back, but let's get going."

"Oh, it's all right," Dana replied. "They can go ahead if they want and we'll catch up. I just want to see this one trail. I think I hear a waterfall."

Jan was in a pickle. She wanted to keep up with the group, but she didn't want to leave her hiking partner.

"OK, you can go down there for just a minute, but I don't want to get in trouble," Jan said as she watched Dana move down the trail.

"There IS a waterfall down there," Dana exclaimed. "I'll bet it's beautiful. Let's ask Mrs. James if we can stop on the way back."

"I don't even want to tell Mrs. James you went down there," Jan replied. "Let's get going and catch up."

They ran up the trail just in time to hear a teammate yell, "TWELVE!" up ahead of them.

Jan yelled "THIRTEEN!" and Dana yelled "FOURTEEN!!" right after, and nobody knew about Dana's little side trip. It would remain their secret…at least for a while.

CHAPTER 3
RUNAWAYS

"OK, un-clip the leash but hold onto your dog's collar," Bryce said.

David Madison was twice Bryce's age and had already been in the Army. But he and his dog Harper, a big German Shepherd, were brand new at search and rescue. Bryce was helping them start out. Despite his young age, lots of adults asked Bryce for help.

"It's not about the searching," Bryce told David. "Your dog was born knowing how to search. We only need to teach him what to do when he finds somebody. We're going to do what's called a 'runaway.'"

Bryce explained to David how the runaway would work. First, David would hold Harper tightly while Bryce teased the dog a little bit. Then Bryce would turn and run down the trail–that's where the name "runaway" came from. When he got around the first corner, he would duck into the bushes, call David on their two-way radio, and say "In position!" That's when David was supposed to let Harper go.

Once Harper found Bryce, Bryce would radio the word "Contact" back to David. That's when the real work would begin. David would need to call Harper back, make him sit, say "Show me," and then run back to Bryce—whether Harper followed him or not.

"We're teaching Harper what's called a 'refind,'" Bryce said. "First he finds the missing person, then he gets you and finds them a second time. That's why it's called a 'RE-find.'"

"Then we party?" David asked.

"Then we party!" Bryce replied. After a dog has done a successful refind, it's party-time. The dog gets a lot of praise and its favorite toy. In the beginning, a dog might search for less than a minute, and party for a full five minutes. This turns the important work of learning search and rescue into a big ol' fun game for the dog.

"You ready?" Bryce asked.

"Yes!" came David's reply.

"Heyyy, Harper!" Bryce teased. "I'm gonna get lost! You have to come find me!" He started backing away from David and Harper, waving his hat to keep the dog's attention.

"Ohhh, I'm getting lost." Bryce turned and ran as fast as he could down the trail. Suddenly he stopped and turned to face David and Harper. One more bit of teasing.

"Haaarrrrperrrr…you gotta come fiiiiinnd me." With that, Bryce went around the corner and out of sight. He trotted a few feet further and then ducked into the bushes.

"In position," Bryce called over his radio. "Release the hound."

David had never seen Harper run so fast. That was good, he obviously liked the game they were playing. But how could a dog use its nose while running at top speed? David tried to keep up, but Harper disappeared around the corner and out of sight.

"Contact! Call your dog!" were the next instructions from Bryce. That meant Harper already found him. David was surprised the dog did it so quickly.

"Harper, come!" David hollered. Search dogs are required to have obedience training, and Harper had already passed that class. He knew what "come!" meant, and ran to David immediately.

"Good dog! Sit!" Harper sat.

Then David gave the next command. "Show me!"

Now, that was a command Harper had never heard before. He didn't know what to do. David took off running toward Bryce, repeating the command, "Show me!" He ran down the trail, and Harper followed, a bit confused. Then the two of them got to Bryce. And it was party time.

"Yay, Harper!" Bryce cried in a high-pitched voice. They gave Harper his ball, and treats, and water, and lots and lots of praise. He got his back scratched and his belly rubbed. They played for almost five minutes.

"I can't believe he found you," David said. "He was running at top speed! How could he be using his nose?"

"Look there on the trail," Bryce replied. "Skid marks in the dirt. He was moving really fast, but when he lost my scent he screeched to a halt. He turned and came right back to me. That was perfect."

"He seemed a little confused about 'Show me,'" David said.

"That's not unusual the first time. Bet he's already got it figured out. Ready to go again?" Bryce asked.

David picked up Harper's ball and put it back in his pocket. He grabbed the dog's collar, and Bryce repeated the teasing and hat waving. Then he ran off down the trail, and David held Harper's collar to keep him from following. Once he was out of sight, Bryce made his radio call.

"In position," came the word, and David let Harper go. The dog ran just as fast as the first time, and quickly disappeared around the corner. He overshot, but he skidded to a halt again, then turned and went in on Bryce.

"Contact!" Bryce called on the radio, but Harper was already headed back to David.

David praised Harper all the way back. "Good boy, good boy, come right on back." Harper skidded to a halt right in front of David and went into a perfect sit.

"Show me!" was David's command, and this time he didn't need to lead. Harper spun out of his sit position and ran right back to Bryce. When David caught up, he threw Harper the ball and started praising him a lot.

"Make this really good praise," Bryce told David. "He did exactly what you want and he needs to know that. Lots of belly rubs, and toss his ball a couple times. He seems to really like playing fetch."

David had been in the army and had won a medal for something heroic and dangerous. But nothing had ever excited him as much as watching Harper learn to be a search dog.

"You're going to be a great partner, little buddy," he told Harper, while rubbing his belly. "We're going to practice and practice, and I know that someday you're going to save somebody."

CHAPTER 4
DANA FALLS

Mrs. James and all 14 of her scouts had reached to the summit of Green Mountain just fine. All were warm, dry and together.

Now the test would be staying warm and dry while they stopped to eat.

While you're hiking, your body is making heat from the work you're doing. When you stop, your body stops producing that heat—and you get cold.

"Okay, girls. You each have extra clothing in your packs–that's one of the Ten Essentials, right? Take off your rain coats, put your spare jacket on and then put your rain coat back on top. That'll help keep you warm while we eat."

The girls did as they were told, and each got out the food they'd brought along. While they ate, Mrs. James peppered them with questions.

"If you do happen to get lost in the woods, what's the most important thing to remember?"

"Stay in one place," Rochelle answered.

"Good," Mrs. James said. "But not the answer I'm looking for."

"Follow streams downhill?" Betsy guessed.

"No. Not all streams lead to civilization. Some just lead to bigger streams that are too deep to wade across."

"Shelter," was Diane's quiet answer.

"I'm sorry, honey, I don't think everybody heard that," Mrs. James responded. "Say it louder."

"Shelter!" Diane tried again. "Shelter is the most important thing. After that comes water, then food."

"That, my dear, is absolutely right." Mrs. James thought that even though Diane was quiet, she was also very smart.

"Girls, here's how this works. You will freeze to death long before you will starve to death. If you get lost, the most important thing is building a shelter. You need to get out of the rain and wind. Let me show you how."

Mrs. James took a lightweight tarp and a rope from her pack. She tied the rope between two trees and threw the tarp over it. She used four small metal stakes to hold down the corners and crawled under the tarp and out of the rain. It made a perfect, upside down V that protected her from the rain. The girls crowded around the open ends so she could talk to them.

"I want everybody to crawl in here, one at a time, and feel how nice it is to be out of the rain. Then pack up your stuff and we'll head home. Everybody still warm?"

"Yess!" they all cried, and each took a turn sitting in Mrs. James' tarp shelter. Then they picked up after themselves so there was no trace they'd ever been there. Finally, they changed out of the extra clothing they put on when they stopped to eat.

"We'll get too hot if we wear all this while we're walking," Rochelle offered.

Mrs. James reminded them to keep each other in sight and to watch the person behind them. That was fine with Dana. Because there was no one behind her and Jan, they wouldn't have to watch anybody. Dana could spend her time watching the woods and looking for animals. She especially wanted to visit the waterfall she heard earlier.

The girls had done so well that day that Mrs. James forgot to do regular checks to see where everybody was. They were more than halfway back to the parking lot when she remembered, and hollered that the girls should count off.

"One." "Two." "Three," came the answers, all the way up to number 12.

But there was no 13, and no 14.

Mrs. James was worried.

"13, you there?" she yelled. She started walking back toward the end of the troop. "14! You there?" Even louder.

Nothing. Just the sound of the rain falling. Mrs. James thought she could hear a waterfall in the distance.

"Girls, let's stay really close together and backtrack to where we last saw them," she said. They got to the hidden trail that Dana had taken before, and Mrs. James wondered if that's where Jan and Dana had gone.

"No numbers now," she told the girls. "We'll all yell at once, and we'll yell their names."

"JAN!!" everyone yelled. They waited a bit to see if they got an answer. "DANA!!!"

Still nothing.

"JANNN!" they tried again. This time they got an answer. "I'm coming!" Jan yelled back. "But I can't find Dana!"

Jan was out of breath when she got to the group. Mrs. James immediately began asking her questions. "What do you mean you can't find Dana? You were supposed to be together."

"I know, but she just took off. She wanted to see the waterfall. I didn't want her to go alone, but I didn't want to leave the group. By the time I decided to follow her, she was gone. I never caught up with her. I heard you yelling and decided to come back."

Mrs. James made a hard decision.

"I want half the group to stay here, and I'm going to leave Diane in charge of you. The rest of us will go down the trail and see if we can find Dana. If she shows up here, don't let her leave. Just wait here till we get back."

Diane knew exactly what to do. She was quiet, but firm. She had everyone open their packs and put their extra coats on, just as they had at lunch. Then she had them rig a shelter just as they'd been shown earlier.

"Dana might be wet, or hurt, when she gets back. She'll need a place to change into dry clothes or wait for more help," she told the other scouts.

"You need to take care of yourselves too," she said. "Drink some water and get a snack. If something bad has happened there might not be time later."

Meanwhile, Mrs. James and the others went down the trail. Over and over again they called Dana's name, but never got an answer. They didn't see Dana, nor any sign of Dana. They looked in the bushes beside the trail, but Mrs. James didn't think they should go too far off the path.

After about an hour of searching, it was obvious they needed more help. Mrs. James and her group went back to where Diane and the others had been waiting. They took down the shelter, put their extra clothes in their packs, and hurried down to the parking lot.

Mrs. James again put Diane in charge. "You all wait here, in case Dana walks out on her own. Set up that shelter again in case you need it." Then she got in her van, and drove five miles to the nearest working telephone.

"Hello, 9-1-1? I'd like to report a Girl Scout missing on Green Mountain."

CHAPTER 5
THE SEARCH BEGINS

Bryce was feeling pretty good about having helped David and Harper on their first day of search and rescue training. Despite the rain and wind, Harper had done well. David seemed to have a knack for working with dogs and because he'd been in the army, David already knew a lot about being safe in the woods. He'd probably teach Bryce a survival trick or two in return for all the help with his dog Harper.

Bryce's cell phone rang, and he could see it was the county sheriff calling. He answered immediately.

"Hi, sir. Is there a search?"

"There sure is. We've got a girl scout missing on Green Mountain. Can you bring Sierra and help out?"

"Of course," Bryce responded. "I'm just finishing training, and my parents are here to pick me up. I'll have them bring me to where you are."

The Sheriff asked Bryce to bring all the other members of his search team, even David. Even though Harper wasn't ready to search for real, David's skill in the woods might come in handy.

It took Bryce's parents about 20 minutes to get Bryce to the trail head parking lot. Because he'd been at training, his gear was already packed and ready to go.

The Sheriff asked him to hurry out before all the other searchers started. "The trail I want you to search isn't printed on the map, but I've drawn it in about here," the Sheriff said. "There's a waterfall nearby, and Dana's hiking partner said she wanted to see the waterfall."

"We'll check that first," Bryce said. "Has anyone else been there?"

"Yes. The scout leader took a few of the girls to try and find Dana. They didn't leave the trail, though. It's steep and slick and they were afraid of getting hurt."

"OK, we'll check the trail first to see if Sierra can smell her. If she can't pick up her smell on the trail, we'll start pushing through the bushes." Bryce got Sierra out of his parents' truck, put on his own backpack, and the two of them headed out. Everyone knew a dog was going into the woods, because Sierra wore a bell on her collar. The bell helped Bryce know where she was, even if he couldn't see her at night or in thick brush.

Sierra could easily tell that a lot of people had walked down the trail. She ran along sniffing the dirt and the bushes. Her nose was picking up a lot of scent- it was the other girls in the scout troop. Every time she left the trail, though, Sierra found nothing.

After Bryce and Sierra had walked for about two hours it started to rain even harder than before. If Dana was still out there, she was probably getting very cold. Bryce knew she had extra clothing, but even that might not be enough on such a cold, rainy day.

Bryce decided it was time to get off the trail for real, and start checking in the woods. That would be harder for both of them, as there was thick underbrush. In some places it came up nearly to Bryce's knees, meaning that it would be hard for Sierra to get through. There were also sticker-bushes that they'd have to go around from time to time.

"OK girl, let's go this way," Bryce said as he made a right turn off the trail. They were now headed directly into the bushes, and Bryce could see the hill get steeper. The rain was really coming down- what the TV weather lady called a "gulley-washer."

Once off the trail, Bryce and Sierra tried to go in a back-and-forth pattern through the bushes. If Dana was too far away for Sierra to smell her on the first pass, maybe as they made other passes Sierra's nose could pick her up.

Then, a snap of Sierra's head! She clearly smelled something and was moving faster now. Bryce tried to keep up, but the hill was very steep. It was also starting to be rocky, and the rocks were wet from all the rain.

Bryce thought they were very close to Dana and was hurrying to keep up with Sierra. He slipped, got his balance back, and slipped again.

"I have to slow down," he thought. Bryce knew if he tried to keep up with Sierra he'd fall. Sierra's job was to go find Dana, then come back and get Bryce. Bryce didn't need to risk hurting himself by rushing, but he was getting more excited.

Bryce lost sight of Sierra. Then she got so far away that he couldn't even her bell ringing. Getting so far from Bryce was always a sign that Sierra smelled someone. In the past, she'd always returned, done her special "sit," and then led him back to the missing subject. But Bryce knew a little girl was in trouble and he wanted to help her as fast as he could.

The third time Bryce slipped he fell very hard. Both his feet went out from under him, and his head hit on a stump. He slid down the hill a ways, pulled by his heavy pack. For just a moment he wondered what had happened, and then he passed out.

About that time Sierra was coming back to Bryce. She couldn't find him at first, but knew what he smelled like. She sniffed and sniffed, and finally found Bryce laying on the hillside just below the rocks. All Sierra knew what that he looked like he was asleep.

For awhile, Sierra licked Bryce's face, trying to wake him up. Then she barked at him. It was a very high-pitched bark, because Sierra was upset. Dogs get upset when they see their master is injured. Sierra could definitely tell that Bryce was hurt.

Sierra and Bryce were very close. Once, when Sierra got sick, Bryce had slept on the floor next to her kennel. She didn't want to leave Bryce, but she could tell that licking his face wasn't helping. Sierra did something that was very hard. She turned away from her master Bryce, and ran back toward the trail.

She was going for help.

CHAPTER 6
SIERRA'S BACK!

There is a strict rule for search and rescue dogs at search base. They are always supposed to be on a leash. This is because there are people and cars around base. It is rude (mostly to the people) and unsafe (mostly for the dogs) to have even a well-trained search dog running loose.

When Sierra showed up at base without Bryce, people noticed. She barked at everyone in a high-pitched bark they'd never heard before. But most everyone assumed that she was just being a playful dog, and wondered where Bryce was. After all, Bryce had always been good about following the rules.

The Sheriff saw Sierra was loose, and called her over. "Hey, Sierra, how's my good girl? Where's Bryce?"

That's when Sierra turned and ran back toward the trail. She ran right in front of a car and almost got hit. The Sheriff caught her and grabbed her collar. Then he led her over to the command van.

The command van was an old school bus. The Sheriff's Office took out all the seats and put desks and chairs and maps and radios inside. It was the place where the Sheriff "commanded" every search.

The Sheriff took Sierra inside. She stopped barking, but was panting and jumping up on the Sheriff. He worked with Bryce and Sierra a lot, and he'd never seen her this unruly. The fact that Bryce was not around was starting to worry him.

The Sheriff turned to the SAR volunteer sitting in front of the two-way radios. "Call Bryce Finn and find out where he is," he said. "And let him know his dog's running loose around base."

The woman picked up the microphone and pushed the button on the side. "Dog 44, this is Command."

"Dog 44" was Bryce's call sign. That was how he knew radio calls were for him. "Command" was the call sign of the Command Van.

No one answered the radio call. She tried again. "Dog 44, this is Command. Do you read me?"

Nothing. "ESAR 57, how about you? Do you read me?"

ESAR stands for Explorer Search and Rescue, a team of Explorer Scouts who didn't have dogs. They searched as a team of four or five people. Bryce's friend Dennis was their team leader, and his radio call sign was ESAR 57.

"ESAR 57 to Command," Dennis said into his microphone. "Your radio's working fine. Let me try calling Bryce."

"This is Command, 57. Yes, please. Try calling Bryce and see if he can hear you."

"Dog 44 this is ESAR 57, do you read?"

"Dog 44 this is ESAR 57, do you read?"

"Command, this is ESAR 57. I'm not getting 44 either."

The Sheriff decided he couldn't wait any longer. Sierra was acting weird and Bryce was nowhere to be found. Something bad must have happened.

He stepped outside the Command Van to find David waiting there. David's German Shepherd Harper was safely back in David's truck.

"I saw Sierra, but Bryce wasn't around," David said to the Sheriff. "Do you need a leash? I've got Harper's."

"I would if we were staying in base, but we're headed back out on the trail. I'm going to see if Sierra will lead me to Bryce," the Sheriff said.

"Can I come?" David asked. "I'm new in SAR, but I was a medic in the army."

Medics aren't doctors, but they're very close. The army gives them lots of first aid training so they can help other soldiers who get hurt. The Sheriff knew David's army training might come in handy when they found Bryce.

"Yes, you can come. Grab your backpack and let's get going," the Sheriff said. "Sierra's about to pull my arm off trying to get back out on the trail."

When they got to the start of the trail, the Sheriff let go of Sierra's collar. She ran as fast as she could to the first bend in the trail and stopped. Then she turned around, looked at David and the Sheriff, and barked her high-pitched bark. When they caught up to her she ran to the next bend, stopped and barked again. She led them down the trail this way, never getting out of their sight.

"This is not good," the Sheriff said to David. "Sierra is really upset. Maybe Bryce is hurt and can't use his radio. Let's try to keep up with her."

Sierra got to the spot that the Sheriff had marked on the map for Bryce. He was not surprised to see her turn and head down the hidden trail. It was the same spot where they thought Dana might be, so it made sense that Bryce would be searching in that area.

A few feet down the hidden trail, they saw Sierra turn into the brush. It all made sense. Sierra was leading them to Bryce.

The Sheriff stumbled, but didn't fall. "Maybe Bryce fell and hurt himself," he said to David. "The brush here is terrible. I've almost tripped three times already."

Sierra continued to lead them as the hillside got steeper, the brush got thicker, and the rocks got slicker. Finally, the dog stopped running. She sat still, barking non-stop.

Did that mean what they thought it meant? Had Sierra led them to Bryce?

CHAPTER 7
She's Gone Again

"Bryce! Bryce! Wake up, buddy!" the Sheriff said loudly.

Sierra had indeed led the Sheriff and David to Bryce, who was just starting to wake up.

"What? Where?" Bryce managed to mumble.

"You must have fallen," the Sheriff said. "You've got quite the bump on your old noggin."

David was the new guy, but he was also a former army medic. He wanted to help Bryce, but he didn't want to just push the Sheriff aside.

"Sir?" he asked. "Can I get in next to you and check him out?"

"Of course, my mistake," the Sheriff said. "You're the one who should be working on our patient." He stepped back from Bryce and used his two-way radio to let base know they'd found him.

David checked Bryce from head to toe. He made sure he wasn't bleeding from a cut they couldn't see, and checked his neck thoroughly. Because Bryce hit his head hard enough to raise a lump, there was a chance he'd also hurt his neck. Neck injuries can be very serious.

Luckily, David found nothing else wrong. He asked Bryce, "Do you know how long you were asleep?"

"No." Bryce's head was starting to clear up. "Where's Sierra? What are you guys doing here?"

"Sierra came all the way back to base and got us," the Sheriff said over David's shoulder. "Your beautiful little golden retriever blew into base and raised such a ruckus that we had to follow her back to you."

"She led you back here? From base? Wow…that's pretty cool. Did you give her the ball?"

David and the Sheriff both understood what Bryce meant. In their hurry to help Bryce, they'd forgotten to give Sierra her reward for leading them to him! David reached inside

Bryce's pack and got Sierra's ball. He tossed it to her, but she just dropped it at her feet. She remained sitting at Bryce's side, watching intently.

"Sierra…good girl! Thank you." Bryce reached out and scratched Sierra behind the ear, which let her know he was okay. She laid down next to him.

"You're nice and warm, girl," Bryce said. "And now that I think about it, I'm kind of cold."

David reached back into Bryce's pack. He took out a pad that Bryce could lay on to get off the cold ground. He also got out Bryce's sleeping bag and draped it over him.

"Bryce, since you got a bump on the head I need to make sure your brain is working right. Do you feel awake?"

"Yeah. I've got a little headache though."

"That's pretty normal," David said. "When you look in the mirror you'll see you've got a pretty good lump just above your ear. Now tell me, how many fingers am I holding up?"

"One," Bryce replied.

"At least you don't have double-vision, which is a good sign. Now, follow my finger with your eyes. Don't turn your head."

David saw that Bryce's eyes moved together. That was another good sign. Sometimes when people hurt their head, their eyes don't move correctly. Now David had to ask Bryce some simple questions to make sure his brain was okay.

"What day is it?"

"Saturday."

"Good. Do you know where you are?"

"Green Mountain, right off a squiggly little line that the Sheriff drew on the map."

"Good again. Who's the President?"

"Obama."

"Three for three. Let's see if you're able to sit up," David suggested. He and the Sheriff grabbed Bryce by the shoulders and gently raised him to a sitting position.

"Whoa...a little woozy. Okay, I'm getting my bearings. I think I'm okay."

The two men continued to prop Bryce in his sitting position. They made sure his sleeping bag was wrapped around his shoulders to keep him warm. They talked to him some more to make sure his brain was working right. He seemed okay. They weren't going to take any chances, though. They'd call another team from base to carry Bryce out on a stretcher.

As Bryce got better, Sierra relaxed. She picked up her ball and began to chew on it. She wandered a few feet away, near the bushes, as Bryce, David and the Sheriff continued their conversation.

After a few minutes, Bryce looked around and asked "Where's Sierra?"

No one had noticed that Sierra was gone. David got up and looked around. He saw her prized rubber ball, laying by the bushes where they'd last seen her. THAT was unusual. Sierra almost never gave up her ball. It was her paycheck for searching.

"She couldn't have gotten far, it hasn't been that long," David said. He walked around the spot where Bryce lay, looking into the bushes, but didn't see her. Then Bryce told him that Sierra was wearing a bell. They stopped and listened, but they couldn't hear anything. Wherever Sierra was, it was far enough away that the three of them couldn't hear her bell.

The Sheriff got on his two-way radio again. "All teams, please keep an eye out for K9 Sierra. Bryce is okay, but while we were working on him she disappeared. If you find her, please keep her with you and let us know your location."

Bryce couldn't believe that Sierra would do something so irresponsible. She'd always been a very good dog, and usually didn't even need to be on a leash. He got very upset. "I'm so sorry, Sheriff. I've made a real mess of this search. I went and got myself hurt, which means you two are helping me instead of looking for Dana. Now my dog has gone and wandered off."

What Bryce didn't know–what none of them knew–was that Sierra hadn't just "wandered off."

CHAPTER 8
MAKING THE FIND

"Don't be too hard on yourself, Bryce. David's headed off to find Sierra, and we'll get her back to you," the Sheriff said.

"It's David's first search! I know he was in the army, but he knows nothing about search and rescue," Bryce replied.

Army medics learn more than just bandaging wounds and splinting broken limbs. They do everything other soldiers do. They especially learn to use a map and compass to find their way around in the woods. Before she disappeared, David had noticed Sierra looking over and over again in one direction. He suspected she'd gone that way.

David took out his compass. Yes, Sierra could have turned and gone another way, but he started walking in that same direction. It was the best chance he had of finding her. The brush was very thick, and the trees kept him from seeing the sun. The only way he knew to keep walking in Sierra's direction was to use his compass.

The map said there was a waterfall ahead. For there to be a waterfall, there had to be a very steep hill. David wondered if that was the kind of place where Dana might have fallen, just like Bryce did. He continued in that same direction, using the pointer on his compass.

The sound of the waterfall got louder and louder, so David knew he was on the right track. He knew that the waterfall was so loud he might not be able to hear Sierra's bell, even if he got close. But that didn't matter. He had to keep looking for both Sierra AND Dana.

Suddenly the tops of the bushes behind him started to rustle. They were very thick, but he could see something was coming toward him. They were also tall, so he couldn't see what was headed his way. All he could see was the brush shaking.

Was it a bear? Was it a cougar? Either of those might try to eat him. He had something called bear spray, which is made from pepper. It stings really bad if it gets in your nose or eyes. Bear spray easily makes a bear or cougar want to run in the other direction. So David got out his spray can. He was ready to spray whatever jumped out of the bushes.

What jumped out of the bushes was Sierra. A clump of leaves was jammed in her bell, which is why David hadn't been able to hear her before. His Army training paid off, and he was calm enough that he didn't use the pepper spray on Sierra. She walked right up to David's feet and sat down in front of him. She didn't jump on him or try to bark. She simply sat and stared at David, right in the eye.

Bryce told me that when Sierra's found someone, she sits in front of him, David thought. I wonder if she's doing that now?

David remembered that at SAR practice, Bryce told him to use the command "Show me!" to tell his dog to lead him to a missing person. Sierra wasn't David's dog, but he figured Bryce probably did the same thing with her. He cleared the leaves from Sierra's bell. Then he gave the command.

"Sierra! Show me!" Sierra jumped up, spun around, and ran toward the waterfall. David did his best to keep up, and quickly realized why Bryce had fallen. The hill was steep, the rocks were slippery and going fast was dangerous.

Sierra's bell was now loud enough that David could hear it over the waterfall. He heard it ringing, then it stopped, then it started ringing again. He realized Sierra was headed back to him, just like his own dog had done at that very first day of SAR practice.

When Sierra got back to David, she barked, then jumped, and ran back a short distance toward where she'd come from. There, on the ground, David saw Dana. She was breathing, but not awake. She had an even bigger bump on her head than Bryce did.

David didn't have Sierra's toy ball with him. He grabbed a stick, waved it a bit, and then threw it over Sierra's head. She immediately ran to grab the stick and began playing with it. That gave David a chance to check on Dana. He could see that she was badly hurt from falling on the rocks.

David used his two-way radio to call the Sheriff. "Sierra led me to Dana, but she's out cold. We need to get her to a hospital as soon as possible."

"The stretcher just arrived to get Bryce out of the woods," the Sheriff responded. "We'll send it to you and get another team to come get Bryce. Where are you?"

"We're right over by the waterfall," David said. He used his compass to tell the Sheriff which way to come from where he was waiting with Bryce. "Have them find the hidden trail to the waterfall, and come down it about a quarter of a mile. We'll be in yelling distance from each other and I'll guide them to me."

When David finished talking to the Sheriff on the radio, he turned and saw Sierra lying next to Dana, gently licking her face. He thought he should make Sierra move. He didn't want her to hurt Dana by jumping or laying on her. But Sierra was being very gentle. By lying right next to Dana, Sierra was also helping keep her warm.

Dana moved a bit. Sierra was licking her face. "Nice puppy," she said softly. "Good doggie…" And then she went right back to sleep.

In very short order, the team with the stretcher arrived at the spot where Dana lay. Right behind, there were some firefighters trained to give first aid. David told the firefighters that the only time Dana woke up was when Sierra was licking her face.

Very carefully, the team got Dana on the stretcher and carried her all the way back to the trail head. Instead of an ambulance, there was a helicopter waiting. They loaded Dana in, and it took off for the big hospital in Seattle.

The only words she spoke the whole time were the words she said to Sierra.

It turned out that Bryce didn't need a stretcher after all. Once he got warm, and a little bit of food in him, the firefighters said he could try walking out. He was slow, but Bryce, the Sheriff and the firefighters all got back to the trail head just in time to see the helicopter leave with Dana.

"See, Bryce?" the Sheriff said. "You didn't make a mess of this at all. Sierra led David to Dana, and she's going to get the best medical care there is over in Seattle. That little dog of yours is one special pup."

Bryce knelt down beside Sierra. He scratched her behind the ears. "Good girl," he said. "You're the best little search dog anyone could hope to have."

CHAPTER 9
REUNION

Dana's parents were worried. She'd been at the hospital for two days, but still hadn't woken up. She'd fallen very hard while trying to visit the waterfall, and took a bad bump on her head.

The doctors did a lot for Dana. They made sure she was warm, and in a comfortable bed. Her parents brought her favorite PJ's, and the nurses helped get the sleeping girl into them. Dana was breathing okay and her heart was working just fine, but nothing anyone did would help her wake up.

Two of the firefighters who treated Dana in the woods dropped by for a visit, hoping that might wake Dana up. It didn't work. Then, the lady firefighter remembered something David said while they were carrying Dana to the helicopter.

"She woke up just once," she said to Dana's mother. "It was when the little search dog who found her licked her face. Dana said something like 'good doggie,' and then fell back asleep."

"That's it!" Dana's mother cried. "Dana loves dogs. If anything was going to wake her up, it would be puppy kisses."

Dana's mother went and got the nurse. "I know if we could bring that dog in here, Dana would wake right up," she said.

It was very much against the rules to have a dog in a hospital. Dana was in a special ward for very sick people, and dogs were even more forbidden there.

But the nurse knew that sometimes, in very special cases, rules had to be broken. She called Dana's doctor, and the two of them talked. They agreed that nothing else had worked, so they'd arrange to have Sierra pay a visit to the sleeping Dana.

The two firefighters were excited and wanted to help. "We'll go get Sierra" the lady firefighter said. "We'll have her back here johnny-quick."

The two firefighters broke some rules too. They weren't driving a fire truck, but they borrowed a car from the fire department office that had red lights and a siren, just like a fire truck. And even though they weren't going to a fire, they turned on the lights and the siren all the way to Bryce's house.

"Get in, quick," the lady firefighter said. "We've got to get you and Sierra to the hospital to see if that helps Dana wake up."

"I wasn't there," Bryce said. "But if David says it worked before that's good enough for me. Let's go!"

Bryce had never ridden in a car with lights and a siren before. Sierra hadn't either. Some dogs howl when they hear the loud noise from a siren, but not Sierra. She just looked out the back window at all the cars they were passing, not understanding why all the other cars had pulled over.

The firefighters glanced at each other during the drive. They were both thinking the same thing. If the Fire Chief finds out we did this...

When they got to the hospital, the nurse was waiting in the lobby. "We moved Dana to a quieter spot at the end of the hall. That way Sierra won't upset the other patients," she said. She turned to Bryce. "She'll have to be on her best behavior, you know. She can't jump on Dana or bump her hard."

"Yes, ma'am," Bryce said back. "We'll be really careful. We'll all lift Sierra on the bed really gently, and she'll take it from there."

And they did. Bryce and the two firefighters lifted Sierra onto the bed as if she were as light as a cloud. First Sierra laid down by Dana's side, but eventually she scooted– gently–toward her shoulder. Then a little more scooting, all very gentle. Finally, Dana's cheek was in range and…puppy kisses!

Sierra licked Dana's cheek. She touched her nose to the sleeping girl's chin. She whined very quietly, as if to say, "Wake up, little friend! Wake up!"

At first, nothing happened. Dana didn't move. But then, a blink of an eye. Dana turned her head just a little bit toward Sierra. "Good doggie," she whispered, almost too softly to hear. Then, "Where am I?"

Dana was awake! Her mother was bursting with joy, but had to remain calm. She didn't want to upset Dana, or cause Sierra to get excited and start jumping around.

"You're in the hospital, honey," Dana's mother said softly. "You bumped your head in the woods. This little doggie found you, and now she's helping you wake up."

Sierra continued to give Dana puppy kisses. Dana scratched Sierra's back. "What's your name, little pup?" Dana asked. "You have the sweetest face."

"This is Sierra," Bryce said. "She's a search and rescue dog and she found you where you fell in the woods."

"Oh, the woods," Dana recalled. "I remember wanting to see a waterfall, but nothing after that. What do you mean she found me?"

Dana's mother took over the conversation. "You slipped and bumped your head, and nobody knew where you were. Sierra used her nose to find you."

Dana's mother did not scold Dana for leaving her scout troop to look for the waterfall. Eventually they'd have to talk about Dana's mistake, but this was not the time. Dana needed to get better first.

"I guess we owe you another 'thank you,'" Dana's mother said to Bryce. "First Sierra found Dana, and now she's gotten her to wake up. That really is a special dog you have there."

"Yes, ma'am," Bryce said. "I'm really glad we could help."

"Dana is learning to bake," her mother said. "What kind of cookies do you like?"

"Chocolate chip, ma'am."

"Well it's settled. As soon as Dana is up and around she's going to bake you the best chocolate chip cookies you've ever had. Tell me–how many people are on your search and rescue team?"

Bryce had to think for a minute. There was David, and Dennis, and the Sheriff, and all the people who'd helped carry stretchers, and the radio operator back at the trail head, and oh my gosh, it was all too many to count! He'd forget someone for sure.

"I'd have to guess, ma'am, but I'd say around 40 people were involved in looking for Dana," Bryce said.

"Okay, 40 it is! The next time you all get together to practice searching, you let me know, and we'll have more than enough chocolate chip cookies for 40 people. Dana will be able to bring them to wherever you're training, and say thank you in person."

"That would be great, ma'am," Bryce said.

"Yes, I can't wait to bake…a thousand cookies…for the waterfall," Dana said. "The waterfallllll…loves…cookies." She was already starting to fall back asleep. After a hard bump, the brain doesn't wake up all at once. Dana had been completely awake for a few minutes, but now she was starting to get sleepy and confused.

"She needs to rest some more," the nurse said. "She'll be awake a little more each day, but this has been long enough for her first day."

Bryce and the two firefighters lifted Sierra off the bed.

"Bye, Sierra," Dana mumbled. She was really getting sleepy now. "I can't wait for more waterfall kisses…and you need some chocolate puppy cookies."

Everyone laughed at the mixed-up words. Even if she was sleepy and confused, Dana was awake and getting better. Sierra had done what the doctors couldn't, and brought the little girl out of her coma.

"Goodbye, young man," Dana's mother said. "I hope you'll come visit us again when Dana is awake enough to enjoy the visit."

"Yes, ma'am," Bryce said. "We'd like that too."

CHAPTER 10
COOKIES

"Wow, these are good cookies," Bryce said. Dana and her mother had come to visit his search and rescue team, and thank them for saving her.

They were out in the woods, where the team always practiced. Everyone was eating cookies and agreeing they were the best they'd ever had.

"Dana, what about the other cookies you made?" her mother asked.

"Oh, right! Where's Sierra?"

"Right here," Bryce said.

Dana got up on a stump and made a little speech.

"I looked in a book, and I found out chocolate is very bad for dogs," she said. "Sierra can't have any of the cookies I made for you all. But I found a recipe for cookies that are safe for dogs, and I baked some of those. Bryce, these are for Sierra."

"Wow...thank you," Bryce said. "I'm sure they're awesome!" He broke one in half, and gave it to Sierra. She gulped it down very quickly, then put her nose up to the sack with the rest of the cookies and sniffed.

"I guess she likes them a lot," Bryce said as everyone laughed.

Dana turned back to the group and continued talking.

"Bryce told me that about 40 of you helped look for me when I got lost and hit my head. You didn't know me, but you knew I was in trouble so you came to help. Just saying 'thank you' doesn't seem like enough, but I don't know what else to say."

"The cookies help!" someone in the back said loudly. Everyone laughed and nodded.

"Dana, how old are you?" Bryce asked.

"12! I'll be 13 in two months."

"Did you know you only need to be 14 to join search and rescue?" Bryce said. "You could come help us find other lost people."

"Oh, wow…that's awesome. Yes…I want to do that. Mom, can I?"

Dana's mother couldn't have been more proud of her. First Dana baked more than four dozen cookies for the SAR volunteers who'd saved her. Then she learned how to bake special cookies for Sierra. Now, she was talking about helping others who were in trouble in the woods.

"If you promise not to fall down and hit your head again," Dana's mother said, "then yes, you can join search and rescue when you're old enough."

Dana and everyone cheered, and Dana told them she'd see them all again when she was 14.

Bryce turned to Dana's mother. "Y'know, ma'am, we take grownups, too."

"Oh, my."

About the Author

Robert D. "Bob" Calkins has been a search and rescue dog handler in western Washington for more than a dozen years. He currently searches with K9 Ruger, a four-year old Golden Retriever who is Bob's third SAR dog. He and his dogs have responded to everything from routine missing person cases, to homicides, to the horrific landslide that in 2014 swept over homes in the tiny community of Oso, Washington.

He is the author of the *Sierra the Search Dog* series of books for children and adults.

About the Real Sierra

Sierra was Bob's first search dog, a Golden Retriever with the well-known "Golden smile" and a natural ability to find people who'd gotten lost. She liked nothing better than running through the woods hoping to pick up the scent of a missing person. Her paycheck was a simple tennis ball, and a scratch on the head. She worked with Bob for five years, responding to many missing person searches in and around western Washington.

CPSIA information can be obtained
at www.ICGtesting.com
Printed in the USA
BVHW04s0525230718
522361BV00005BA/18/P

9 780997 191110